Sara Savage is a social cognitive psychologist. She was based at the University of Cambridge for her doctoral work in 1994 and worked there as a researcher until 2022, when she formed IC Educational Ltd. She is co-founder of the IC thinking approach and has authored 37 publications on preventing social polarisation and extremism along with three popular-level books. IC thinking interventions developed by Sara and her colleagues have been delivered in twelve countries in schools, communities and displaced person camps, to address a wide range of extreme thinking, with statistically significant results. Sara's background in dance and the arts has influenced the writing of The Pack is Back, her first children's book.

In honour of Kim and her children, Aidan, Nathanial and Audrey.

Sara Savage

THE PACK IS BACK

AUSTIN MACAULEY PUBLISHERS™

LONDON * CAMBRIDGE * NEW YORK * SHARJAH

A CIP catalogue record for this title is available from the British Library.

ISBN 9781528922982 (Paperback)
ISBN 9781528922999 (Hardback)
ISBN 9781528963985 (ePub e-book)

www.austinmacauley.com

First Published 2023
Austin Macauley Publishers Ltd®
1 Canada Square
Canary Wharf
London
E14 5AA

Sincere thanks to child education specialists, Sarah Walker and Michele Walker for their insightful work on the Parents' Guide at the end of this book. Michele Walker bravely hauled armloads of tactile teaching materials and stuffed dogs to pilot *Pack Is Back* in a multi-cultural school in South Africa, the birthplace of the dogs' ancestors, and location of story seven. Kind friends and colleagues have been astute and supportive readers: Julie Miller, Lisa Shemilt, Emily Savage, Carrie Pemberton Ford, Alex Ward, to name a few. Many thanks to Dr Crister Nyberg and Maria Krupska for background research informing the Teachers' Guide.

The three chocolate Labradors who star in this book are credited for teaching their owners the way of the pack through the real-life events recounted in these stories. My husband Mark Savage is not only co-pack leader, he also spent hundreds of hours finessing the book illustrations with his graphic and IT skills.

Preface

Did you know that dogs have Super Powers?

Dogs can see in the dark. Dogs can hear a sound from far far away. Dogs have Super Noses and can smell the tiniest smell.

Dogs speak to each other and to us. They use smells to leave messages: I woz here.

They bark to say: Watch Out! It's the Postman! Or, hey, I'm bored!

They waggle their tails and their bodies to say: Let's Play!

They lift their paw to say: Let's be friends.

Dogs can learn up to 120 human words. And like us, dogs dream when they sleep.

Through these true life stories you will learn about how each dog sees the world in their own special way, and how each dog speaks their own special message.

Prologue

When we were born, we were "One Litter" with "One Mother".
  As puppies, we were taken to separate homes.
  Apollo went to one home. Persie to another. The One Pack family was lost.
  Apollo tells this first story.
  Everything in all the stories really happened, just as it is told.

Story 1

Apollo Meets Persie

We were born in the glow of summertime.
We snuggled in a pack with our mother.

You can count how many we are.

My name is Apollo.
My coat is brown like chocolate –
Red brown.

This is my sister Persie.
Her coat is black like midnight –
Blue black.

We are two puppies for sale.

One day I am taken to a new home.
I am the only dog here.
Where is my mother?
Where is my sister?
Where is my pack family?

I spend my first night alone in my box.

I am very brave.
(I cry a little.)

The next morning, I am too shy to go out and play.
The garden is too big.
I stay safe in my basket.
I gaze out at the big strange world.

I discover that my little legs run so fast!
I zoom from the bushes to the fence.
I whoosh from the fence to the bushes.
My puppy legs zig and zag across the grass.

Birds see me, and their wings flap.
My Pack Leaders' hands clap.
I am a small dog, a lonely dog, but boy, I am fast!

It's time to go to puppy class.
I sniff the air. My nose is excited by the puppy smell.
I scramble into the room.
My legs splay out, my paws skitter. I slide into the room on my tummy.
'Pleeeeease – I want to play with the puppies!'
I waggle and sniff and greet each one.

Is this my pack family?

During class, I show off to the puppies.
Look! I can do all the tasks: "Sit, down, stay".
I am so clever.
Most of all, I love the puppies.
My wagging tail says, 'Please, will you please join my Pack?'

My human Pack Leader sees my longing. I place my paw on her head.
She understands.
Soon she brings home a new puppy to join my pack.

Guess what!
It's my sister, Persie. She needed a new home.

I haven't seen her for so long.

I remember her smell. I like chasing her in the garden.

We roll and wrestle and sniff and chase.

My pack is back!

Uh oh. There is a problem.

My pack leader cuddles Persie too much.

I feel angry when Persie gets all the attention.

Hey – I was here first.

I want my pack leader to love me the most.

I growl. I snarl.

I try to scare Persie away.

At bedtime, we touch noses to make-up.

Dogs never stay angry for long.
We lick our paws clean as we climb into bed.

But the next day, I growl and bark.
My barking says:
'It's not fair! I was here first!
I am the **Special Number One Dog**!
Persie – go away and don't come back!'

My pack leaders don't understand.
They cuddle Persie too much.
My head snaps away.

My eyes will not watch.
My throat growls my complaint.
My raised fur says, 'Beware, watch out – I'm really upset.'

I place my bottom **firmly** upon my favourite patch of grass.
This says to Persie: 'This grass is MINE.'
When I get up, Persie pees on my patch, saying, 'This grass in now *MINE.*'

I **hate** Persie.
She is trying to steal my place.
My lips snarl.
My puppy teeth flash – *sharp, sharp*.
My paws pounce and chase Persie away.
Her eyes are wide with fear,
her tail between her legs. *Ha ha.*

My pack leaders grab me and tie my lead to a tree.

They shout at me: NO Apollo! **Bad dog, Apollo**. Bad dog!

They shut me in the kitchen. All alone.

Whooooo hoo hoo hooo, I wail.

Don't leave me here by myself.

I am your Special Dog! I was here first.

My paws scratch at the door. *Scritch scratch Scritch scratch.*

It seems Persie is the favourite now.

No one wants **me** anymore.

What shall I do?

I do what I can. I speak from my heart.

I send a dream

to tell my pack leader the problem.

My dream says: **I am your special dog.**

I will bother Persie until you treat me as your Number One Dog.

Finally my pack leaders understand.
They learn to pet me first, feed me first, as they should.

Then it is Persie's turn.

This pack has rules.

I was here first.

Now Persie and I can play *together*.

No matter how much we eat for dinner – we always want more.

Our puppy rules say, **never** steal *each other's* food, because that's not fair.

Our puppy rules also say:

But you can eat the humans' food, as long as they aren't looking.

Chomp chomp.

We puppies are polite, and we have OUR way of keeping OUR rules.

If I get mad at Persie, my head turns away,

and my paw has a good old scratch at my ears.

'Let's change the subject,' my scratching says.

So we can be friends again.

We have learned to walk on our leads. Our pack leaders take us to the fields.

The smells of the world call to us. Our noses are so happy.

Our bodies, strong as horses, pull so hard on our leads.

Finally they let us run free.

We chase an owl and a swan on the river.

We sniff a rabbit hopping away.

You can see us in the distance,

Running, flying, soaring…the best of friends.

We hear our pack leaders call us home.

Our tails waggle in the hope of dinner.

After eating, I curl up by the fire, safe at our pack leader's feet.
The twinkling stars call out to Persie:
'Come out, come out to play with your moonlit shadow.'

She dances for the shining moon.

I have a secret. Shhhhh – don't tell anyone.
Here it is:
Persie is bigger and stronger than me.
She wrestles and pins me to the ground.

But puppies are polite.
We have OUR rules. I am still the Number One Dog.

Here is our Rule Number One – this pack stays together.

Here is our Rule Number Two – whatever happens, good or bad,
this pack dozes together on the big bed...every morning as the sun peeps in.

(post script: The name Apollo is from a Greek story about the god of light and healing.
The name Persie is from a Greek story about Persephone, who like a seed in winter goes down into the earth to be born anew as flowers in spring.)

Story 2

Persie and Apollo Move House

*One day when Persie and Apollo were one year old, their life changed when they moved house. **Persie** tells this story in her own special way.*

I am Persie.

Persie Strong Legs. Persie Long Tongue.

Joyful, Playful, Persie the Clown.

This is my sister Apollo.

Apollo Loud Growl. Apollo Boss Boots,
Apollo Soft Heart and Cuddle Coat.

We have lived four seasons: summer, spring, autumn, winter.

We are one year old – with the bounce and gleam of young teens.

We wonder – what is the pack doing today?
Our nose takes us to where the action is.
Our bottoms sled down the stairs, *rumble rumble rumble.*

Our paws skitter into the kitchen *click click click*
Our legs race into the living room, *whhhhoooshhh*
Our bodies slam into the table, *thump thump.*
There are boxes everywhere, big and chewy.

Our teeth like to tear them up.

People come in. People go out.
We jump up on these strangers so that we can smell them.

They swoosh us away.
They carry away the boxes.
They carry away the big couch.
They roll up rugs and take down curtains.
They remove our beds and bowls.
Our toys are snatched away.

Our place is empty now.

Our toys are all gone. Where are they?
We dig for them in the garden.
We find an old sock, buried in the ground.
Apollo hogs it for herself.

I want this sock.
My throat rumbles like a train *Rrrrrrrrrrrrr*
My body slinks towards Apollo… slooooowly
My teeth *snatch* that sock. *Ha!*

Apollo rages like a storm. *GRRRRRRRRRRRR ROAR*
I oppose her like a tank.
Our most angry fight erupts.

We can't help ourselves.
We can't stop ourselves.
Our jaws and claws can only tear, fight and bark.

Our pack leaders shout – **'Stop it! Bad dogs!'**
We are put away into separate rooms.

Has our fight broken the pack forever?

It is time to get into the car.

We are sad to leave our home.
We say goodbye to our river.
We say goodbye to the geese flying overhead.
Our place grows small as we drive away.
I remember that sock, so nice to chew.
My tongue longs to go back.

Finally, we come to a strange place, a new home, far to the north.
My nose sniffs the interesting smells. (Cows! Fields! Horses!)
Look – a rabbit springs across our path.
Apollo bursts from her lead.
Her legs chase like lightening.

Our pack leaders shout, high and shrill.
'**Apollo, come back**!' they yell.

Apollo knows the meaning of those human words.
But she doesn't listen. She doesn't obey.
Our pack leaders blow their whistle.
They blow it loud and long 'FWEEEEEEEEEE'
But Apollo is gone.

Oh, well… I wonder…if Apollo is *gone*… well then… I can be Number One.
I look up at my pack leaders.
Their faces are white, their eyes afraid.
I know what to do. I thump my paws on their chests.

I speak from my heart: **Send ME!**
My nose can smell Apollo's tracks. My legs can run so fast.
It is my job to protect the pack!

They send me off: 'Find Apollo! Bring her back!'
Off I zoom. My nose skims the ground. My paws race so fast.
My nose zigs and zags, steering by Apollo's scent.
These fields, these trees, these stones – all are strangers to me.

But onwards I go, head down, nose in charge, heart pounding, paws seeking. My legs do not rest to watch a cow.

My nose does not stop to sniff a mouse.

Only one thing matters – catching a hint of Apollo's smell.
My nose leads me to the darkest wood.

There she is.
Snuffling into a rabbit hole.

I lunge at Apollo. My jaws clamp around her collar.
I drag her out. I push her with my nose.
I chase her back across the fields.
Barking at her all the long way home.

Our new place calls out to me so that my nose can find it.
Finally, we come inside. I see my water bowl.
My legs fold. I drop to the floor – too tired to drink.

Our pack leaders hug us and cry out: 'Thank you, Persie! Good girl Persie!
Apollo, don't you ever run away again.'

Apollo knows she did wrong.

She knows she broke the rules.
She rolls over, baring her tummy,
paw lifted, saying, 'I'm very sorry'.
She slides through our leaders' legs, round and round their legs she goes, asking,
'Please, **am I still your Special Number One Dog**?'

Yes, she is.
Apollo licks my ears. I am special too.

That night I have an important message.
I send my pack leaders a dream.

I will protect you. I will protect the pack.

Apollo and I don't fight so much now.
We have come to this new place *together*.
We mark it with pee as our own.

51

We each have our own tasks to do.

Outside the new house, I guard our fences, and patrol our place with a bark.

Inside the house, Apollo enforces the pack rules.

Her new rule is to walk two steps behind our pack leaders.

Apollo the fuss-pot prods me with her nose if *I* disobey.

Our rule number one says:

This pack stays together.

Our rule number two says:

Every dog has a special job to do.

Story 3

Apollo and the Big Dog

A few months later, Persie tells this true story about what happened when Apollo met the Big Dog.

I leap over Apollo.
She soars over my back.
Our friends watch and cheer.
We are the highest leaping dogs on our street.

The sun is setting…
It spills red and gold over all our world.

The late summer hills are calling to us – COME!

We jump up and down, begging our pack leaders – 'Pleeeeease – Let's go walkies!'

Off we go to the rustling woods – running free like the wind.

Look – a big dog runs towards us.

Apollo loves every dog – she meets and greets with the biggest dog smile.

I am a bit shy.
I hang back and watch.
This dog is huge.

This dog's fur is standing up.
This dog snarls.
This dog bares sharp teeth.
From far away, our pack leaders call.

Their whistle blows, Fffweeeeeeeeeee
This means – come back!

The whistle blows twice more. FWEEEE FWEEEEEEE
This means – come back NOW!

I look at Apollo.
She is frozen in the glare of the Big Dog.
This dog is angry
This dog has no collar
This dog has no pack leader
This dog has no MANNERS!

The Big Dog lunges at Apollo and clamps down on her leg with huge sharp teeth.
Apollo struggles to get free. The Big Dog shakes her back and forth.
She fights back with her claws – she fights for her life.

I hear the whistle blow loud three times
FWEEEEEE FWEEEEEE FWEEEEEEE
This means,
COME BACK THIS INSTANT!!!

What do I do?
I want to obey the whistle. I want to run back.
But, the pack should never leave a dog in danger.

I hear the whistle blow four times,
FWEEEEEE FWEEEEEE FWEEEEEE FWEEEEE!!!
This means – **WE ARE WORRIED. COME BACK NOW!!!**

My paws rush back to our pack leaders.
They are talking to each other *Yabba yaddle doodle, yaddle.*
They keep talking *Yabba yaddle…*
I whine
I whimper.
They don't listen to me.

I curl up on the ground and cry.

The one who feeds us stops her yabbing.
She hears my whimper.
She marches into the dark woods.
She blows her whistle LONG and LOUD and SHRILL
FWEEEEEEEEEEEEEEEEEEEEEEEEEEEEEEEEEEE

The Big Dog is scared away. Whooosh – it runs right past her.
Where is Apollo?
The woods are silent.
The sun goes down.

There in the distance –
stands a familiar dog-shape – not moving.

Our pack leader runs to her.
Apollo sees her coming, and falls to the ground.
Her fur is all torn

Her back legs look wrong
Blood pours down, staining the ground.
I am not allowed to lick it.

Our strong pack leader comes running.
He lifts Apollo and carries her through the woods.

We bundle into the car.
We drive through the black of night.

Apollo makes no sound.

We come to the place of strange smells (*vet surgery*)
Strangers take Apollo from us.
They place her on a table to fix her wounds.
'We will work on her all night,' they say.

We say goodbye to Apollo,
We try not to cry.
We drive home to an empty house.

Two days pass.
Our pack leaders come home with an odd-looking dog.

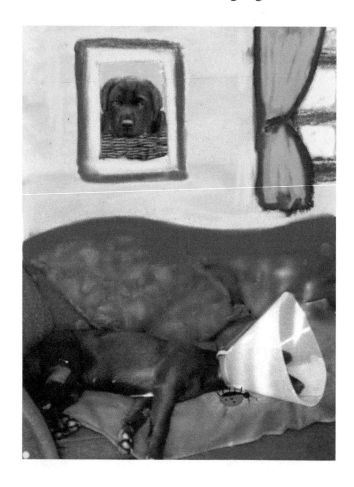

This dog is brown like Apollo, but with a big funny white head.

This dog's fur is shaved off.
This dog smells strange – like the place of strange smells.
This is '**Not Apollo**'!

My head snaps away.
I glue my bottom to the floor.
I will not look at '**Not Apollo**'.

This dog cannot run.

This dog is carried up and down the stairs
to sleep on the big bed.
This dog is brave when her wounds are washed,
but wails when our pack leaders leave the room.

Hey – this dog gets all the attention.
I want to sleep on the big bed too!

My job was to protect the pack –
but the pack is broken.
My tail curls under.
My ears hang low.
I sink to the floor, paws covering my eyes.
I have <u>not</u> done my job.

Then…one day, I am curious.

My nose sniffs inside the strange white cone.
It smells like Apollo in here…
I am not sure who this is…
So…
I sniff her bottom.
Guess what – **IT'S APOLLO!**

I leap into the air!

Apollo is back!
I will make a new effort to guard the pack.
I **will** do my job again.

Now I bark LOUD to tell my pack.
Listen! I say:
Arf! Someone is at the door
Arf! There is a noise in the garden
Arf! It's time for our dinner

Arf! Arf! It's TIME TO TICKLE MY TUMMY!

Today, at the place of strange smells,
there is a different big brown dog.
Apollo sees it. She freezes.
Her body shakes, her heart pounds.
She needs my protection.
Our pack leader lifts her up.
We come home.
Finally – no more bandaged legs. No more big white cone head.
Just white scars, healing nicely.

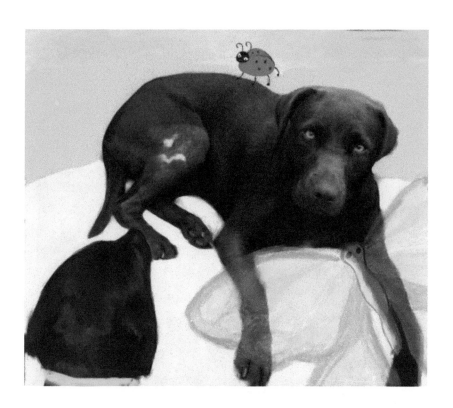

The next day, a dog comes to our house to visit.
Uh–oh. This is **another big dog**.
But this is a friendly dog, with soft curling fur.
A big yellow dog with soft manners. A dog named Truffles.
She plays gently with Apollo.

Apollo cannot run – she hops and limps.

I watch carefully.

I let Apollo play.

I keep watching.

Apollo is learning to tell a good dog from an angry dog.

The pack is learning to be safe.

The pack is back together.

I have done my job.

Story 4

Persie and Apollo Grow Up

Apollo and Persie are now fully grown (two years old). Apollo tells her story about how she discovers her own special talent.

When I was a puppy
I was a grumpy puppy.
A jealous puppy.
Now I have Persie to play with.

We love to wrestle.

Persie pins me to the ground.
Our tails wag for joy.

Today, by accident – Persie hurt my leg – the leg with the special scars.
It hurt. I yelped.

When it hurts, I remember the **Big Dog**

My body starts shaking.

I crawl into my bed.

I hang my nose and ears and paws over the edge.

My sadness hopes to be noticed.

I used to jump so high.

But my legs are not good at running anymore.

Persie licks my ears to say 'Sorry'.

She did not mean to hurt my leg.

Dogs like to forgive each other.

The next day, our pack leaders take us to the hills.

I am not allowed to run.

Persie gets to run free into the woods.

Two little barking dogs rush to greet me – '*ark ark ark ark*'.

Persie leaps out of the woods

She flies to protect me.

Persie the protector crouches down between me and the little dogs – barking so
fierce –

RUF RUF RUF RUF RUUUUUUF.

(I wasn't *really* scared of the little dogs).

At home, we stand side by side.

We are both nearly full grown.

(Shhhh – don't tell anyone. Persie the protector is now taller than me.)

Even though I am small and can't run, I have an important new job to do.

My job is to be a 'Therapy Dog'.

That means I visit people who are lonely.

I go with my pack leader on Sundays, to a place with tall, tall fences.

Even Persie cannot jump over these!
The gates unlock and lock CLUNK CLUNK.

We walk down the shiny halls.
My paws go sliding on the slippery floors. Sssshhhhww wooosh
Heavy doors slam behind us. THAM BAM

Inside there are big men. Tough men.

Some have marks and piercings.
Some have scars – like me.
Did they meet the **Big Dog** too?

I can smell how they feel. They smell afraid.
They smell sad.
I used to smell like that.

Some of the big men are shy.
So, I do not charge at them like a Big Dog.

I come softly, as a friendly dog, a tender dog.
First I lie down on my side, to show my tummy.
I do this to tell them: **Don't be afraid**. *Selah.*
I weave myself under their arms.
and through their legs.
Round and round I go, under the bridge.
My nose comes close to sniff them.
My tongue gently licks their hands.

They start laughing.
They stroke my glossy fur.
I gaze at them with my golden eyes.
I show them my special scars.

'What happened?' they ask.

My pack leader tells them
How I met the **Big Dog** who was angry
How I was hurt
How I could not move
How my pack leaders found me
How they took me to the place of strange smells
How I was brave
How I had to wear a funny white cone

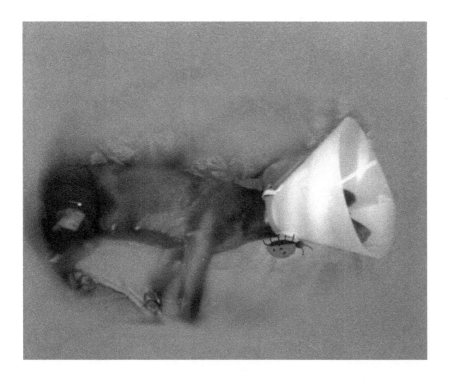

How I got better after a long time
And how I learned to be friendly again – even with big dogs as long as they have
good manners.

The big men look at me with new eyes.
They can see that I am their friend.

My pack leader gives the men a soft toy to throw:
'Fetch!' they say.
I chase the toy and bring it back to them.
That is how I tell them: 'Good throw, well done'.

The big men smile at me.
I am full of sunlight. My eyes beam with golden light.

My wagging tail says how happy I am to make them happy.

Yes, I am a Therapy Dog.

I help people who, like me, have met a **Big Dog**.

I let them feel my soft warm fur.

I do my job.

Persie also wants to be a Therapy Dog.

Her legs race down the shiny hall. Her paws skid into the room.

She jumps up on the Big Men.

She runs in circles, barking loud: RUF RUF RUF RUF

She slurps their faces with her long tongue.

The men shuffle away, their backs to the wall.

TIME FOR PERSIE TO GET ANOTHER JOB!

Back home, we all agree:

Persie's job is protector of the pack.

She is on duty day and night.
She shows off how loud she can bark.

Persie does not have scars that show.

Not like me.
I have **special** scars.

But Persie remembers when she was a puppy and had no home.
She worked hard to join my pack.
I was jealous and tried to chase her away.
She took my lashings and proved her worth.
She has become the protector of the pack.

We are both good dogs. And we are good in different ways.
I am a tender dog.
Persie is a bouncing dog.
Sometimes we play gentle.
Sometimes we play rough,
Either way – we are never far from **mischief.**
Here is how we plan it:
I hide in the tall grass.
Persie runs past me and I pounce.

I ambush her – *'Surprise – Ha Ha!'*
When I am tied to my lead, Persie races past me so that I chase her.
The lead goes YANK around my throat.
Persie turns around to watch – *'Ha ha!'*

At bedtime I show my love
to my pack leaders who saved my life.
I bring them my stuffed toys and cuddle up at their feet.
But in all the world of trees and birds and clouds and thunder,
Persie the Protector,
is my very best friend.

Story 5

Persie's Story

Persie, now three years old, tells her true life story.

I am the happiest dog, with the highest leap.

I love my pack.

I protect them every day.

That means I bark **A LOT**. RUF RUF RUF RUF RUUUUUUF.

That is what I say to postmen, dogs, and especially to C-A-T-S.

I have a good, sharp bark.

Everyone can hear it.

It is a cold dark winter morning.
The sun barely shines and I wake up sad.
The day is full of rain and frost and gloom.

My sister Apollo is sleeping late.

Her wiggling lips, her snuffling snorts,
her jiggling paws show she is running free in her dreams.
Yes – let's go chase rabbits!
My nose nudges my pack leader, pushing her hand to open the door –
'Let's go running in the fields.'

Out come our two leads and the whistle.

It's time for WALKIES!

Apollo hears it and yawns awake.
She stretches her back legs and arches her back.
We both shake our bodies to say out loud – it's time to dance and celebrate the hunt!
I rush up and down the stairs. I prance with joy.
Apollo joins in – we stir each other up – ready to run.

The fields are covered in hard frost.
Our paws crunch through ice, sinking into puddles beneath.
SQUISH SPLASH SQUISH goes the cold muddy water.

Off we go – running towards the hills.
Two dogs, side-by-side, faster than the breeze.
FWEEEEEEEE goes the whistle – this means 'COME BACK.'

I run back to my pack leader…but…
Oh LOOK! – a bird flies past.

My paws turn round and zoom to chase it.
My body flies across the field.
My legs leap over the highest fence.
Onto a busy road.

CRASH.

A big car.
Has it hit me?

My legs keep running, though the world has changed and grows fuzzy around me.

My legs keep running, though I know not where – and my head is spinning.

My legs keep running, though I hear my pack leader shouting.

My legs keep running, though I am slowing, slowing, slowing down

My legs – they buckle

My paws – they stumble

My nose gently meets the cold wet ground.

My body lies there panting, gasping…

I hear my pack leader shouting, shouting: **'Persie Persie Persie!'**

I remember my name.

I remember my pack.
I lay there waiting.

She finds me in the tall grass.
She kneels down close so that my nose can smell her.
She strokes my face and says,
'Persie, Persie, I'm here, I'm here.'

The world softens around me.
My eyelids flutter, my eyelids close.
All is quiet.
All is still.
I can rest now.
My last breath joins the misty air.

My pack sees my strong body lying still upon the ground.
They know that I am no longer there.

Their eyes are crying. Tears stream down.
Their noses are wet.
They snuff and sniffle.
They cry and snuff, and cry again.

Inside the house, Apollo searches for me.
She looks under the bed. She peers into the closet.

She stares at my empty bed, asking:
WHERE is Persie? WHERE?

A gaping hole has ripped the pack.

Our neighbours bring red flowers.

My pack leaders put them where my body lies buried.

They stand in a circle around my grave.
They sing a song.
The sound is pretty.
My strong pack leader says a prayer.
My leaders bow down.
Apollo crouches on the ground.

They stand up and tell my stories like songs.
Songs about **ME, Persie**:

Who found Apollo when she first ran off,
who barked so loud to protect the pack,
who opened doors thumping paws on the latch.
Who jumped for joy at the leads for the hunt,
who danced with delight in the cold moonlight,
who could leap with ease over the highest height.
Who nuzzled your hand to say, 'Thank you so much,'
who enjoyed a tummy tickle, back wriggling on the ground,
and said, 'Amen' with a lick from her tongue.

My stories are so good.
But my pack leader is so sad.
The morning light is hard for her to bear.
She hides under blankets, dimmed like the winter sky.
And Apollo curls up into a tight lonely ball.

I see this sadness from afar.

I send my pack leader a dream. I speak from my heart.

I tell her:

'Don't be sad.

My life was full of love and joy.

I had **love**, because I love my pack.

I had **joy**, because running on the hills was my greatest joy.

But, I am worried about two things:
Will Apollo be lonely without me?
And who will do my job? Who will check that the fences are secure?'

Over the next days, some new things happen.
Apollo, the Sad-Alone Dog,
jumps for joy when the lead comes out. Just like I did.
She stirs herself up for the run. She rushes up and down the stairs.
She performs the dance to celebrate the hunt.
Just like I did.

When a cat slinks by, Apollo now barks for me:
RUF RUF RUF RUF RUUUUUF.
Just like I did.
She checks the fences for me.

Just like I did.

This is a new Apollo, a "Persie-Apollo" –
who remembers all that I showed her to do.
My pack leaders smile to see my work.

I think about this – how Apollo watched and learned from me.
How it was **my** job to protect the pack.

I have done my job, and now I have passed it on to **her**.

Where am I now?
In Apollo, I am inside the pack with the gaping hole.
I also watch the pack from afar.

Maybe you can see me
if you gaze with your heart
at the cold night sky
you might see me dancing in the bright moonlight.

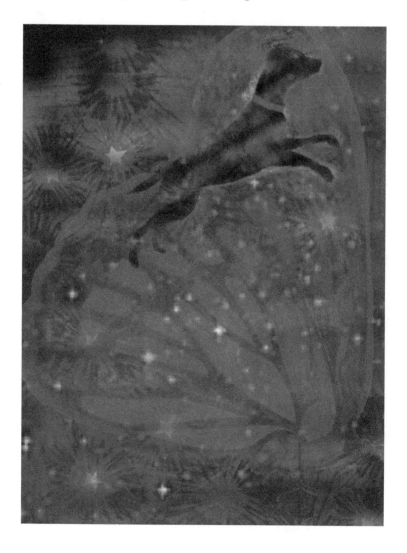

You might see me – Persie – with my shining coat
dark as midnight
leaping high from star to star.

Story 6

Costa comes to stay

When we were born, we were "One Litter" with "One Mother".
As puppies, we all went to separate homes. The one pack was lost.
And now the grieving pack has a gaping hole.
Persie and Costa recall the time Costa needed a new home.
(Costa is so named because she is the colour of a warm cup of coffee).

Far to the south lives a big chocolate Labrador named Costa.
Costa lives side by side with Changa.
Changa is the pack mother who gave birth to Persie, Apollo and Costa that sunny day three years ago.

Changa is old now, but she can still leap over an eight-foot fence.
Costa follows her, they clear the fence like an arc of water.

One day, Costa's human family moves house.
Costa is too bouncy for the new house. She jumps too high. They cannot keep her.
Where will Costa go?
Will she end-up on the streets?
With no food? No bed?
No pack leader?

Everyone agrees that Costa should come to live with us –
the grieving pack with the gaping hole.

Shouldn't the sister Labradors be re-united?

Maybe it will help the pack to heal.

On the day that Costa comes to stay, a cold winter wind blows.

Costa is taken from her mother and led into our car.

The sky is dark as our car drives off.

Costa's body shakes with fear in the back of the car.

Hailstones hit like noisy stones.
Thunder crashes and lightning flashes on the long journey north.
Costa's nose snuffles her blanket with its musty Changa smells.
Her paws dig at the car floor, trying to go back home.

When Costa arrives at our northern fields,
a tiny rainbow peeks through the dark grey clouds.

The moment has come.
Our strong pack leader leads Costa to meet Apollo out on the field.

Apollo sees a familiar shape – a Persie-shape!
Apollo leaps for joy, her tail twirls the happiest twirl.
She races towards the Persie-shape. Wild horses could not stop her.
She nuzzles and snuffles.
Sniff sniff sniff goes Apollo's nose.

This dog smells *a bit* like Persie.
But wait.

This is not Persie.

Apollo's legs back away. Her head turns away.
Apollo will not look at "**Not-Persie**".

Then Apollo's nose remembers, this dog smells like the day we were born –
when we were "One Litter" with "One Mother!"
Apollo's nose remembers – this dog is our **sister,** from so long ago.
Apollo's tail starts twirling again.

A shy double rainbow glows in the dark winter sky.
The two dogs walk together, careful to stay in step.
Careful not to offend.

Is the pack back together?
Maybe so. Maybe not.
Back home, Apollo notices that Costa is a **Big Dog**,
a chocolate brown dog with yellow eyes,
bigger and stronger than her.

Apollo is wary.
A line of fur on Apollo's back stands up. It makes her look bigger.
Costa sees it, and growls a low, rumbling *grrrrrrrrrr* in reply.
A line of fur stands up along Costa's back too.
The air between them is like frost.

Apollo watches while her pack leaders pet nervous Costa.
Apollo's head snaps and looks away.
She cannot bear to watch this wrong display.

Uh oh.
The old problem is back.
Apollo is a jealous dog, a frowning dog.
She wants to be the Number One Dog and get all the love.
You see, our pack leaders' love is like food – we always want more.
And maybe there won't be enough for us all.

Costa wants our pack leaders' love too.

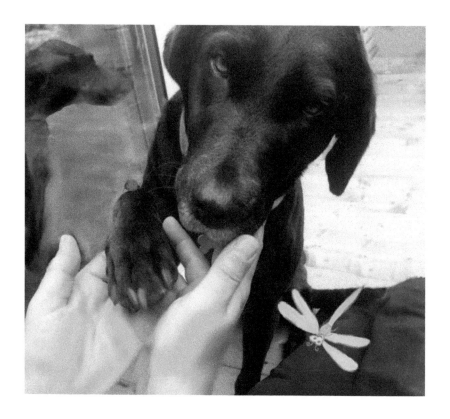

She noses her way on to our pack leader's lap.
Costa lifts her paw and gazes with all her heart.
Stroke stroke stroke goes our pack leader –
petting Costa's velvet fur.
Lucky lucky Costa. Getting all the love.
Giving a thousand licks in return.

Now who will be the Special Number One Dog?

Lonely Apollo wants a new pack-mate – BUT – she insists on being the Number
One Dog.
Costa wants to be loved by her new pack leaders – BUT – she also wants to be
friends with Apollo.
It's a tug of war!
How will it end?

Here's how Costa tries to make friends:
She crouches down. Her bottom arches up.
Her paws thump the ground, saying:
'Let's play Apollo! Let's romp.'
Big, strong Costa pounces on Apollo.
She chomps on Apollo's leg
and shakes her back and forth, saying
'Aren't we having FUN?'

Apollo jumps onto the couch. Her back leg hurts.
Her head snaps and looks away.

That is how she stops the rough and tumble play.

Watching this from afar, suddenly I see…
Costa is a Big Dog – like me, Persie.
Like our Mother Changa…
Apollo is much smaller…
That's it!
Apollo was the runt of the litter!
All of us bigger puppies pushed her away so that we got more of our Mother's milk!
No wonder Apollo was a jealous puppy
and scared by the Big Dog.

Here comes a **really** big problem:
When Apollo cuddles our pack leader at feeding time,
big Costa barges in and pushes Apollo away.
Just like our very first days.
Big Uh oh.

These two dogs have a really big problem.
Who can solve it?
These dogs will have to figure it out for themselves.
Next day, a new thing happens.
Apollo ignores her pack leader.
She pretends she doesn't want to be petted.
Apollo leaves a space – **so that Costa can barge in**.

Costa sees Apollo's generous move, and lifts the paw of friendship in return.
When Apollo jumps onto the big bed, Costa slips off, saying:
'After you, O Number One Dog'.

And if Costa is locked out, Apollo whines till the pack is back.

In return, Costa **never** enters a room
unless Apollo signals with a royal paw, 'Yes, come in.'

Their tug of war is ended by this give and take.
Both dogs are polite.
Both give something up.
In return, both dogs get **most** of what they really want:
Costa gets to be a pack member with Apollo as her friend.
Apollo has a new sister and is still Dog Number One.

The pack rules work!
Both dogs waggle their bodies 'til their ears go *flap flap flap,*
They shake off their anger, they shake off the past.
They say *'the end'* to their upset,
and agree their truce,
with a loud double sneeze.

(Did YOU know that dogs are so clever that they solve problems this way?)

These dogs love to hear that they are 'gooooooood'.
Their ears lift and their eyes close in bliss,
when they hear that human word.
And both dogs are good in different ways.
Costa's legs are good at running like a train.
Apollo's legs are good at running in twists and turns,
though sometimes she limps.
Costa the hunter loves to **chase down** small animals.

Apollo **loves** small animals as though they are her puppies.
She carries her stuffed toys proudly in her mouth,
and tucks them into her bed at night.

The pack is back – and now it's time for WALKIES!
Out come the leads. Costa's eyes blaze bright.
Apollo and Costa shake themselves and race up and down the stairs.
They stir themselves up for the hunt.
Over the fields they race.
Costa's gaze is glued onto Apollo, her packmate;
they run as one.

They plough through the high summer grass. Butterflies leap into the air.
They rush under hedges. Birds screech and flap away.
They soar through the woods. Rabbits jump up and flee.

And who is leader of the hunt?
It's Apollo out in front –
the jealous puppy, the wounded dog,
the small-ish Labrador with the tender heart –
Apollo leads the way.

Story 7

Changa's Tales from Africa

Changa tells a story about the dogs' ancestors who lived in southern Africa long long ago.
(PS Changa is the name of the dogs' pack mother. Her name means 'Value' in the click language called Xhosa.)

The pack hears that Changa, the mother of Persie, Apollo and Costa, has become old and ill.

Costa and Apollo travel south to visit Changa.

Costa hates car journeys, and her body shakes.

Apollo sees it, and allows big, strong Costa to huddle near her on the back seat.

Finally, they arrive.
It is dark, and the moon is full.

Costa's eyes shine with joy to see her mother Changa, lying on her bed.

But her nose can smell that her mother is not well. Costa restrains her wagging tale.

Both dogs crouch low around Changa's bed.

Changa awakes from her fitful sleep.

Her nose remembers the scent of her grown-up puppies.

Here is her small chocolate puppy, Apollo.

But where is Persie, her shining black puppy?

Oh, and here is her favourite, Costa, who grew up so close by her side.

How Changa misses leaping those high fences with Costa following right behind.

Costa lifts a loving paw, and drapes her velvet ear upon Changa's bed.

Changa moves stiffly on her cushions.
Even in her old age Changa's black coat gleams.
Only her white paws and muzzle show that she has lived twelve long years.
(Each dog year is like seven human years, so Changa is like someone 84 years old).

Changa's time is running out, and she must teach her grown-up puppies one last lesson.
And so Changa recounts the tales that were told to her, *Tales from Africa*:

'Long long ago, before there were roads, houses, or even dogs,
our ancient ancestors lived in Africa.

Our ancestors were wolves!

The wolves lived in packs guided by special rules:

- *This pack stays together.*
- *Every pack member has a special job to do.*
- *Respect the Number One Dog.*
- *Stay away from angry animals.*
- *Have fun, play rough, but be polite.*
- *Give and take to maintain the pack peace.*
- *Dance and stir yourselves up for the run.*
- *Work together as a team for a successful hunt.*
- *Don't fight over food – share it with the whole pack.*
- And here is Changa's favourite rule:
- *Doze together in your comfy den every morning as the sun peeps in.*

'My puppies, do you recognize these rules?'
'Yes,' say Apollo and Costa, their strong tails wagging back and forth – 'those are the rules we live by!'

'Yes,' Apollo shouts, 'like the time Persie leapt out of the woods to protect me from the little barking dogs…'

'Yes,' says Costa, waggling her ear with the fresh red scar,

'Like when Apollo and I fought over that bag of food.

Apollo won, but we shook off our fight

and marked our truce with a loud double sneeze.'

Changa is glad that her puppies have remembered what she taught them –

licking them when they obeyed,
and swatting them with her paw when they didn't.
She is proud that her puppies are keeping the pack rules,
even though they live among humans with their strange human rules.

Her work is nearly done.
Changa stretches and groans. Its hurts when she moves.
She must hurry on with her lesson:

'Long ago, our ancient family, the wolves
spread across the lands of Africa.
They spread north and south, east and west.
They spread far and wide across the world because they knew how to live by the
pack rules.

Meanwhile, the climate of the world changed,
and the first humans walked around the tall African grass in search of food.

They were smart and invented stone tools and fire.
The humans needed to become good at hunting.
But they didn't know how to hunt in a team like we do.

They didn't understand the wolves' pack rules.

And the humans didn't know that a pack can include members beyond its own kind.'

'I wonder how humans and wolves first became friends?' asks Costa.

Changa breathes deeply and says, 'Maybe some hungry wolves smelled food the humans were cooking over a fire.

The smell was so delicious – the wolves couldn't help it – they crept closer and closer.

Maybe a human child threw them a scrap of food.

And the wolves came back every day.

'So often, the humans came back from their own hunt empty-handed.

Maybe the humans wanted to learn from us how *we* hunt.

Maybe the humans watched the wolves as:

- The pack stayed together
- Every pack member had a special job to do
- The Number One wolf led the hunt
- The fastest wolves ran like the wind
- The smartest wolves circled ahead to corner the prey
- Then all the wolves shared the meat with the whole Pack – the puppies, the mothers, and the old and wounded too.
- Then the pack rested together in their comfy den.

Soon the humans tamed some wolves and hunted with them in a team.
Was it the humans or the wolves who first said, 'Let's adopt these others into our pack?'
It happened so long ago – no one knows for sure.'

Changa's voice is a whisper as she struggles to explain,
'Over time, the tamest wolves had pups that grew up gentle,

becoming like dogs.'

Apollo asks, 'Like *tender* dogs?'

'Tender but strong,' rasps Changa.
'Some of these ancient dogs had a ridge of stand-up fur along their backs.
These dogs were called Ridgebacks.
They have lived in southern Africa for hundreds of years.
They were so strong and smart that together they could corner a lion, and still can do so today.
That is why they are also called Lion Hunters.'

'Lion Hunters?' gasps Apollo.
'Yes, Apollo, my smallest puppy with the Special Scars.
You too fought your own battle, with "lion paws" and great courage.
Just like your Ridgeback family on the grassy plains long ago.'

Changa struggles on with her tale:
'In those days, our Ridgeback dog family hunted with the tribe called **Khoi** –

which means "the people".

The moon was the people's guide, showing both dogs and humans the times for hunting.

The Ridgebacks and Khoi revered the moon
with all her faces, from full to crescent thin.

When the moon was full, together the humans sang and the dogs howled an almighty song,

'O beautiful moon
O pitted moon
who takes the hits
as the sister moon
and protects the Earth and us all.'

Costa and Apollo sit still in wonder.

Changa's voice is faint as she finishes her tale.

'Humans are our pack leaders now.

They share their food and shelter with us.
We must protect them in their time of need, and obey their rules to live well in their world.
Though long ago our ancestors first showed humans our way.'

Changa raises herself up to tell her offspring one last thing,
'I am Changa, your mother.
I am half English Labrador and half African Ridgeback.
See – I have a ridge of stand-up fur along my back.
Each of you, my mixed breed puppies, also has that ridge of stand-up fur.
Wear it with pride.
Like your Ridgeback family, you are strong and intelligent.
You must never forget that **you are from the wild**.
To avoid fights, you must be good pack members – and live by the eternal pack rules.'

Changa drops down stiffly onto her bed, her lesson ended.

Costa noses her way forward, to be close to her mother.

Apollo bows low to Changa.

Our pack leaders crouch down too.

A ray of moonlight peeps through the window.

The pack waits together in silence.

Changa's laboured breathing slows down…wanders off…to a far…far…distance…and is heard no more.

Costa and Apollo lay their lonely muzzles on their pack leaders' knees.

The sound of the African night rustles in Changa's ears.

She hears the crickets thrumming, the insects whirring, the grasses rustling.

She is drawn by the starry African night and the moon that watches over all.

The southern night sky blazes with families of stars –

constellations of stars – leaping dogs,

wild dogs, tame dogs,

dogs and humans from every part of the world.

Look! – two shadows slide across the moon.

Are those wind-blown clouds?

Or Persie and Changa chasing a shooting star?

End

Parents' guide

Part 1. Game Activity for children **ages 4+** – **before** you read the stories

(Note: Parents' Guide Part 2 and Part 3 for children **ages 6+** is placed **after** the stories.)

Peek in advance

1) Can you find the ladybird and butterfly in pictures in Stories 1–4?

   Count how many ladybirds there are in Story 1.
   (Story 2, Story 3, Story 4)
   Count how many butterflies in Story 1.
   (Story 2, Story 3, Story 4)

2) Can you find the dragonfly in pictures in Stories 6, 7?

In picture 6.8 there are many ladybirds, butterflies and dragonflies. This picture shows a summer day in the natural world – with all the creatures leaping and flying together. Can you find the owl, the rabbit, the birds?

3) What is the main colour for the:

	answer:
Butterfly? _____	*(blue)*
Ladybird? _____	*(red)*
Dragonfly? _____	*(green)*

4) What <u>colour</u> is the dog collar for:

answer:

Persie? _____

(blue)

Apollo? _____

(red)

Costa? _____

(green)

5) Which insect belongs to which dog?

Prompt: Aha! Blue collar, blue butterfly. Red collar; red ladybird. Green collar, green dragonfly.

answer:

Butterfly belongs to_____

(Persie, black Labrador, blue collar)

Ladybird belongs to _____

(Apollo, chocolate Labrador, red collar)

Dragonfly belongs to _____

(Costa, chocolate Labrador, green collar)

The insect is a symbol of each dog's personality!

6) Have you heard of the term 'spirit animal' or 'avatar'?

Each dog has their own symbol, their own avatar.

7) What is the avatar doing in the pictures in story 3? In story 4?

Sometimes the avatar copies what the dog is doing. Sometimes the avatar is being alongside the dog, or just having fun. What do you think?

138

8) I wonder why Persie's avatar insect is a blue butterfly?

You can think about this as you read the stories. Maybe because Persie can leap up high into the air like a butterfly? Maybe because her coat is a blue-black colour? What do you think?

I wonder why Apollo's avatar insect is a ladybird? Maybe because Apollo can sometimes be gentle and polite like a ladybird? Maybe because her coat is a red-brown colour? What do you think?

I wonder why Costa's avatar insect is a green dragonfly? Maybe because Costa is a big dog who runs fast in the fields, darting like a dragonfly? Maybe because her eyes are yellow-green? What do you think?

Part 2. Parents' Guide for children ages 6+

The purpose of this guide is to explore thoughts and feelings sparked by the stories, and to promote social and emotional intelligence.

There are no wrong answers to any of the questions. Throughout, affirm your child's engagement with the stories. Enjoy!

How to use:
Read the story together, and invite conversation:

- Exploring the main question
- Viewing the picture (page number provided).
- *Further prompts are in italic.*
- Ideas to support your child are in the right-hand column.

If extra support is needed

- If a child needs extra support at any point, spend more time listening to the child's thoughts and feelings. Th support ideas provide realistic comfort.

- Next, gently switch the child's attention to finding the dog's butterfly, ladybird or dragonfly in the pictures related to the issue at hand.
- Next, point to the picture at the end of the story concerned, and ask the child to describe what she/he sees in the story's final picture. (Hint: point to any positive or lovely elements without closing down the child's exploration.)

Story One. Apollo and Persie

1) How did Apollo feel when she was taken to a new home? See pictures 1.4, 1.5.

Have you ever moved to a new home? Or a new school? How did you feel?

> Support. It's OK to feel sad or anxious when we are lonely. Apollo's sadness did not last too long. She loved going to puppy class where she made new friends. See picture 1.6.

2) When Apollo met her sister Persie again, how did she respond? See picture 1.7.

What do you think it means when dogs touch noses?

> Support. When you like someone, how do you show it? Sometimes we hold hands, smile, laugh and play together. What other ways can you think of?

3) Uh oh. How did Apollo feel when she saw her pack leader giving Persie lots of attention? See picture 1.8

Have you ever felt like Apollo did?

> Support. Sometimes it is hard to explain why we are feeling angry or sad to others. Apollo

140

kept trying to show her feelings. See pictures 1.11, 1.12.

4) Which dog superpower did Apollo use to finally show the pack leader how she was feeling? See page x about dog superpowers. See picture 1.13.

Apollo was determined to be understood. Have you ever kept trying to explain your feelings?

Support. Apollo waited for a quiet time, when she was not feeling so angry. She spoke from her heart, and 'sent' her message to her pack leader. In a dream, her pack leader finally understood.

5) How did Persie and Apollo show they have become friends? See pictures 1.16, 1.20.

Have you ever made up with someone after a fight? How did you feel?

Support. It can be hard when we 'fall out' with our family or friends. We may feel sad and lonely. But like Persie and Apollo, we can learn to say sorry to each other and not stay angry for long.

Story Two. Persie and Apollo Move House

1) How did Persie and Apollo feel when their house was emptied? See picture 2.5.
Have you ever had to move from a home or school? How did you feel?

Support. It can be hard when we say goodbye to a special place, and we may feel upset and worried for a time – until we make new friends and make the new place our home.

2) Why did Apollo and Persie have a big fight? See pictures 2:5, 2.6

Were the dogs feeling scared and upset because all their toys were gone? Their beds were gone?

Support. The pack leaders put Apollo and Persie in different rooms so that everyone could cool down. Even though it was a big fight, the two dogs knew deep down that they needed to stick together.

3) What did Persie do when Apollo did not obey the pack leaders' whistle calling her back? See picture 2.8, 2.9.

Like Apollo, have you ever broken a rule at home or school – not thinking about what you were doing? See pictures 2.11, 2.14.

> Support. Good rules are there to keep us safe. Apollo broke the rules because she loves to chase rabbits. She ran off – not thinking, not listening.

4) Persie knew she needed to help Apollo and the pack leaders. Have you ever acted bravely to help someone?

Has someone ever helped you like that? (See pictures 2.9 to 2.13)

Which dog superpowers did Persie use to find Apollo and the way back to home?

> Support. Persie's super-eyes could see in the dark woods and her super-nose was able to find the way home. Persie is like a best friend or family member who never gives up till she does her job. See picture 2.14

5) Apollo knew she did wrong. She says sorry to the pack leaders. What did the pack leaders say to Apollo? See picture 2.15.

Is Apollo still the number one dog?

Support. Yes, the pack leaders love her, and she is still their special number one dog.

Persie is special too. Persie realises that has a special job to do – she is now the 'Protector of the Pack'. See pictures 2.17, 2.18.

Story Three. Apollo and the Big Dog

1) Apollo loves all dogs – and she runs to greet the big dog in the woods. See picture 3.3. What signs were showing that the big dog was an angry dog? (Hint – see story on page x)

Not everyone we meet always wants to be our friend. Has anyone ever been unkind to you? How did you feel when that happened?

Support. It would be normal to feel alone and scared, and to look for support.

Who could you turn to for support if someone was mean to you?

Unlike Apollo and Persie, the big dog did not have pack leaders to teach him how to be a good friend to others.

2) Persie sees that Apollo is in danger. She also hears the pack leaders' whistle blowing, again and again. What should Persie do?

Has there ever been a time when you felt torn between two choices, and did not know what was the best thing to do?

Support. Persie knew she had to obey the pack leaders, even though she did not want to leave Apollo in danger. Persie then felt terrible because the pack leaders did not understand the real problem (see picture 3.4). Persie kept on crying until the pack leaders realised something was wrong. They searched for Apollo and took her to get medicine (see picture 3.5). Sometimes doing the right thing takes several tries. Persie persisted until it turned out OK.

3) Apollo looked different when she came home from the place of strange smells (the vets surgery). How did Persie react to the 'strange looking dog'?
(See picture 3.6)

What dog super-power did Persie use to finally recognise her sister?

> Support. Sometimes the people we care about get sick and need special care. We can feel sad to see those we love change and look a bit different. We might be needing more attention too. When Persie realised that Apollo really had come back – she leapt in the air! (See picture 3.8)

4) Persie regains her role as Protector of the Pack. She allows the new dog to play with Apollo. See picture 3.11 Can you remember the big lesson the pack learned?

(hint: The pack is learning to be safe, learning to tell a good dog from an angry dog).

> Support. After something bad like the attack in this story happens, after something bad happens like the attack in the story, it would be normal never to befriend another big dog. But Persie feels she can allow this new big dog to play with Apollo because she can tell that this dog is a kind dog with gentle manners.

Story Four. Persie and Apollo Grow Up

1) What did Apollo do when Persie accidently hurt her leg with the special scars?

How did Apollo show that she felt sad and wanted attention? See picture 4.2.
What are some of the ways you show someone that you are feeling sad?

> Support. Sometimes accidents happen and people can hurt us even though they don't mean to. Similar to Apollo, feeling hurt now can lead to us remembering something sad in the past. Talking to someone we trust is one of the ways that can help us feel better when we think about sad memories.

2) What is Apollo's important new job? See picture 4.4

How did Apollo help the big men to feel better?

> Support.
> Apollo felt sad and frightened after the big dog had hurt her. She could see and smell that the big men also felt sad and afraid. Even though she still could not run, she showed them her special scars and let them stroke her glossy fur.
> Have you ever helped someone who was feeling sad? What are some of the ways you helped them feel better?

3) Persie and Apollo are both good dogs and they are good in different ways. Why do you think Persie is better at being a Protector than a Therapy Dog?

Has anyone ever told you that you are good at something? How did you feel hearing that?

> Support. Sometimes we may not understand why we haven't been chosen to do something. Persie wanted to do the special therapy-dog job that Apollo had been given, to be exactly like

145

her sister. But the pack leaders could see that Persie was perfect for being the Protector of the Pack. And just like Persie and Apollo you are special in your very own way.

4) Persie and Apollo sometimes play rough and sometimes play gentle. They have become best friends. See picture 4.9.

Do you have one or two favourite friends?

<u>Story Five. Persie's Story</u>

1) What were some of the things that Persie loved doing? See picture 5.1

What are some of the things that you like to do, that make you happy?

> <u>Support.</u> Persie did what made her happy, like leaping, eating, barking and getting tickled. As you grow, you too will discover more about what makes you happy and what special tasks you will like doing.

2) How was Persie feeling when she woke up on that cold dark winter morning?

The day was full of rain, frost and gloom. Have you ever woken up and felt this way too?

> <u>Support.</u> Even though Persie was the happiest of dogs, she could also feel sad. There are many reasons why we might wake up feeling sad. Sometimes it is hard to understand why. It's OK to feel that way and to remember that not every day is the same.

3) What happened when Persie heard the pack leaders' whistle calling her back? See picture 5.3

Can you think of a time someone in your life was trying to stop you from doing something that you wanted to do – so they could keep you safe?

Did you find it hard to listen to them?

Support. The pack leaders blew their whistle because they didn't want Persie to run off. At first Persie listened to the whistle and came back. But then she wanted to chase the bird flying over the fence. She did not understand how close she was to the dangerous road. It all happened so fast.

The pack rules and the whistle were meant to keep her safe. Even though sometimes we may not understand the rules, they are there to keep us safe.

4) It was a terrible shock when Persie was hit by the big car. Have you ever felt how the pack felt when this happened to Persie?

Perhaps losing someone or something very special to you?

Support. It feels very sad when we lose someone we love. The pack leaders loved Persie. They showed their grief in different ways. The pack leaders cried, their noses and faces streaming wet. Apollo curled up into a lonely ball, as life turned grey without Persie. See picture 5.8

Apollo was grieving too, and searched for Persie. See picture 5.5. It's OK to show others how we are feeling. Kind people will help to support us.

5) How has the pack changed? See picture 5.6.

Can you see a dog-shape in the cloud in 5.6? Why do you think this picture is torn?

What did the pack leaders say and sing as they remembered Persie's life and what they loved about her? (hint: look at page x)

What are some of the ways you remembered someone or something that was special to you?

Support: When we lose someone it is so hard to understand why. We feel so sad. The pack leaders told stories and sang songs to help them remember Persie. There are many ways to remember we have love about someone: photographs, videos, telling their life stories.

Persie sent the pack leaders a dream to help them not feel so sad. She reminded them that her life had been full of love and joy.

6) By springtime, how did Apollo, the sad-alone dog, begin to change? See picture 5.9.

Can you see how Apollo checks the fences, just as her sister Persie used to do?

Support: Even when people we love have died, what they have given to us stays inside us forever. Persie's lessons were now inside Apollo, and now it was Apollo's turn to protect the pack and remember her sister with love.

Look at the last picture 5.10. Can you imagine seeing Persie leaping high in the cold night sky? Can you also see Persie's avatar leaping with her?

Story 6. Costa Comes to Stay

1) How did Costa feel leaving her mother Changa, to start a new life? See picture 6.2

Have you ever had a big change in your life that meant you were away from home?

> Support. Changes can be very difficult and can make us feel worried and afraid. Costa remembered the comforting love of her mother Changa by snuggling into a blanket with her smell. This helped her to feel less afraid during the long journey.
> Have you ever brought something with you to a new home or school, that helped you remember happy times?

2) How did Apollo react when she first saw Costa out on the field? See picture 6.3.

What dog superpower helped Apollo remember that Costa is her sister from long ago?

> Support. Apollo used her super nose to recognise her sister Costa, even though it had been such a long time since she had seen her. The double rainbow in the sky was a sign that brighter days were coming.

3) When Apollo comes home with Costa, she notices that Costa is a big dog who wants all the pack leaders' love. See picture 6.4. How do you think Apollo felt?

What did Apollo remember that made her feel sad? Look at picture 6.5.

> Support. Apollo remembered the fight with the big dog and how frightened she felt. She also

remembered that she was the smallest puppy in her dog pack and how the other puppies pushed her away so that they got more of their mother's milk. We can understand why Apollo tends to be jealous.

5) Here is their problem:

Costa wants the love of her new pack leaders and she wants to be Apollo's friend.

Apollo wants a sister, but she must be number one!

Have you ever had a tug of war between your feelings?
Maybe you had to share the love of special people in your life with others?

Support. Feeling worry, jealousy, wanting attention, competing, feeling sad are all normal feelings. It looks like Apollo felt all these things, and had bad memories too, tugging her in the opposite direction from her desire to have a sister again.

6) How do the dogs solve their big problem? From page x:

"Apollo leaves a space – so that Costa can barge in...
Costa sees Apollo's generous move, and lifts the paw of friendship in return.
When Apollo jumps onto the big bed, Costa slips off, saying:
'After you, O Number One Dog'.
Their tug of war is ended by this Give and Take.
Both dogs are polite.
Both give something up.
In return, both dogs get most of what they really want:
Costa gets to be a Pack member with Apollo as her friend.
Apollo has a new sister and is still Dog Number One." Look at picture 6.8.

Support. Bringing Costa home brought up a lot of mixed feelings, and Apollo went back to her old ways – being a jealous, frowning dog. But dogs are very clever and they figured out how to solve their problem. They both gave something up and in return got what was most important to them. The Pack is Back! – together they race over the fields as one.

7) Guess who becomes the leader of the pack? See picture 6.9.

Do you know anyone who is a bit like Apollo? – one who starts out grumpy but learns to become a loving person and a kind leader?

Support. "Apollo, the jealous puppy, the wounded dog, the small-ish Labrador with the tender heart – Apollo leads the way." Apollo discovered that she could be a good leader of the pack. She overcame her feelings of jealousy so that he could help others.

Story 7. Changa's Tales from Africa

1) How does Apollo help her sister Costa on the long car journey to visit their pack mother Changa? See picture 7.1

Support. Apollo could see her sister's body shaking and allowed her to huddle near her. Even though Costa is the bigger dog, she needed the tender heart of Apollo to comfort her. The pack rules mean that they know how to look after each other.

2) Can you name the animal that long, long ago were the pack's ancient ancestors?

Hint. See picture 7.3. Ancestors are members of our family who lived long, long before we did. They have passed their intelligence and strengths down to us.

Support. The dogs' mother Changa helped them to understand how in ancient times some wolves became friends with humans, and over a long, long time grew tame and eventually became dogs.

3) Changa tells her grown puppies that their pack heritage is part English Labrador and part African Ridgeback Lion Hunter dogs. (No wonder Costa, Apollo and Persie are so smart and can leap so high!)

Do you know where your family comes from?

Hint: Long, long ago, your own family may have lived where you live now, or they might have come from a different part of Britain, or Europe, or the Middle East, or Africa, or Asia. Your ancestors have passed on to you their intelligence, strengths and skills.

Support. You can talk with older members of your family to hear about your family's tales.

Do you have friends that come from different parts of the world?

You can ask them about their family's tales and heritage too.

4) Can you name Changa's favourite pack rule? (Hint: see picture 7.4.)

Can you name some of the other pack rules in this 7.4 picture?

Support. The pack rules were created long ago by the pack's ancestors, the wolves. Changa had passed on the lessons she had learnt to her puppies when they were young. These had stayed with them as they grew and helped the pack work together.

Can you think of a rule in your life that keeps you safe and happy?

5) Can you find pictures throughout the seven stories that show the wolves' and dogs' pack rules in action in Apollo, Persie and Costa's lives?

Hints:

1. This pack stays together
   See 1.20, 4.9, 6.6

2. Every pack member has a special job to do
   See 2.9, 2.16, 2.17, 2.18, 4.4, 4.7, 5.1

3. Respect the Number One dog
   See 1.13, 1.14, 6.8, 6.9
   1.17 (obeying the whistle of the human pack leader)

4. Stay away from angry animals
   See 1.19, 3.3, 4.2

5. Have fun, play rough, but be polite
   See 2.3, 2.4, 3.9, 4.1, 4.8

6. Give and take to maintain the Pack Peace
   See 2.15, 6.6, 4.9

7. Dance and stir yourselves up for the run
   See 1.16, 1.18, 5.1, 6.8

8. Work together as a team for a successful hunt.
   See 1.17, 6.3, 6.8

9. Don't fight over food – share it with the whole pack
   See 1.15, 7.4 (this shows Costa *after* a food fight!), 7.6

10. Doze together in your comfy den every morning as the sun peeps in
    See 1.20, 4.9

What **new** rules do the dogs need to obey to live well in the human world?
See 7.10

Hint: Obey the whistle! Don't run off. Don't bark too much. Don't chew the furniture.

In her last moments, Changa was hearing the sounds of her African
heritage calling her home. What were those sounds?
Hint: think of a hot summer night with gentle wind blowing, insects…

Support. If you have ever had to say goodbye
to someone who was special to you, what
sounds might help you to feel peaceful when
you think of that person or pet? (sounds of
waves, river flowing, wind, bird song…)

6) Look at the night sky with Costa and Apollo. See 7.11.

What episodes of the dogs' ancient and present-day life stories can you see in the constellations of stars?

Please place this Part 3t Guide after Story 7 – eg after all the stories have
been read.

Part 3. 'Big Picture' Questions Guide
after reading all the stories

For children aged 6+

1) Quickly look at the stories from Stories 1-7.

Challenge: Look for **gradual change,** from the story 1 to story 7, in the
pictures of avatars/ insects.

Hints:

- *Notice how the drawings of the insects start out like a scribble (page x) and become clear and simple like a child's vivid drawing when the dogs are puppies,*
- *Next, they become rich with many colours and more complexity as the dogs grow up.*
- *When the dogs are adults in stories 6 and 7, their avatar/insects and the natural world are all 3-D and realistic!*

The way the avatars/insects change over time are a symbol of the dogs growing up.

2) Now look at the picture backgrounds in stories 1-7.

Challenge: Look for **gradual change** in the picture backgrounds (inside the house, outside in the natural world), from story 1 to story 7.

Hints: how the dogs see the world changes as they grow up:

- *As puppies in stories 1 and 2, notice how the drawings of inside the house and the natural world start out clear and simple like children's drawings when the dogs are puppies.*
- *As growing dogs in stories 3,4, notice how the houses and the natural world of the dogs become rich with many details and colours. The sky, sun and clouds also show more complex details as the dogs are growing up.*
- *As adult dogs in stories 5,6,7, notice how the natural world is shown as it looks in photographs – 3-D, realistic, detailed, with perspective and a single light source linking the whole picture together.*

The dogs' **understanding of the world** 'grows up' over time.

Humans go through this kind of change over time, from **seeing the world** as toddlers, to seeing the world as older children, and then seeing the world in full 3-D realism. (As children grow up, their drawings illustrate this change.)

In each stage, the world has its own special beauty.

Social and emotional learning teaching resources using The Pack is Back stories for Primary Schools and for teaching children who are out of school are now available.

Discover online visually-rich classroom resources for the Pack is Back. Visit www.IC-EDU.org